ANGRY BIRDS®

A SIDE-SPL[...]
RIB-TICKLING J[...]

D0497581

CHEEP LAUGHS

EGMONT
We bring stories to life

First published in Great Britain 2012 by Egmont UK Limited
The Yellow Building, 1 Nicholas Road, London W11 4AN

ISBN 978 1 4052 6657 4
54817/6
Printed in Great Britain

BIRD BANTER

WHICH ANGRY BIRD LOVES BOOKS?
Red.

?

WHAT DO YOU CALL A GIANT ANGRY BIRD?
A weapon of mass destruction!

WHAT DO YOU CALL AN ANGRY BIRD WITH A HEADACHE?
Level 2.

WHAT DO YOU CALL AN ANGRY BIRD WHO'S JUST HAD AN ANGER MANAGEMENT CLASS?
A bird.

WHAT'S THE BEST MARK A CLEVER BIRD CAN GET AT SCHOOL?
E – for Egg-sellent!

!

WHY DO THE ANGRY BIRDS LOVE DESTRUCTION?
Because it's so egg-citing!

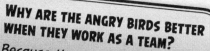

WHY ARE THE ANGRY BIRDS BETTER WHEN THEY WORK AS A TEAM?
Because they egg each other on!

WHAT DO YOU GET IF YOU CROSS A TIGER WITH A KANGAROO?
A stripy jumper!

WHAT SOUND DOES AN ANGRY BIRD HEAR WHEN IT FALLS OFF A CLIFF?
An Egg-ho!

WHAT'S YELLOW AND GOES WHEEEEEEEEEEE-BANG!
Yellow bird.

WHAT DO YOU GET IF YOU CROSS AN ANGRY BIRD WITH A PIG?
Lots of mess!

FEATHERED FROLICS

WHY DON'T DOGS MAKE GOOD DANCERS?
They have two left feet!

WHERE CAN YOU FIND MOZAMBIQUE?
On the Mozam-bird.

WHY DID THE CHICKEN CROSS THE PLAYGROUND?
To get to the other slide.

WHAT DO YOU GET FROM A BAD-TEMPERED SHARK?
As far away as possible!

HOW DO YOU STOP A PIG FROM SMELLING?
Put a peg on its snout!

WHY DON'T POLAR BEARS EAT PENGUINS?

They can't get the wrappers off.

WHAT KIND OF SNAKE IS GOOD AT MATHS?

An adder!

WHY DID THE MUDDY CHICKEN CROSS THE ROAD TWICE?

Because he was a dirty, double crosser!

WHAT DO AN EAGLE AND A LION HAVE IN COMMON?

They both have wings ... except for the lion.

WHAT DO YOU CALL A WOODPECKER WITHOUT A BEAK?

A headbanger.

WHY ARE SEAGULLS CALLED 'SEAGULLS'?
Because if they flew over the bay they'd be bagels!

WHY DID THE BIRD FLY UNDER A RAINCLOUD?
It was feeling under the weather!

WHAT DO YOU CALL A HUNDRED PENGUINS WITH SUN BURN?
Lost!

WHY DID THE PARROT WANT TO BE THE BOSS?
It liked to suck seed!

WHAT HAPPENED TO THE COLD JELLYFISH?
It set!

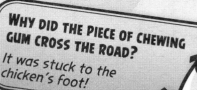

WHY DID THE PIECE OF CHEWING GUM CROSS THE ROAD?
It was stuck to the chicken's foot!

WHAT DO YOU GET IF YOU RUN OVER A BIRD WITH A LAWNMOWER?
Shredded Tweet.

WHAT DO YOU CALL A GIANT CANARY?
Sir.

WHAT DO YOU CALL A SLEEPING BULL?
A bull-dozer!

WHY DO BIRDS FLY SOUTH FOR THE WINTER?
Because it's too far to walk.

SIDE-SPLITTERS 2

WHY IS A GIRAFFE'S NECK SO LONG?

Because its feet smell!

RED BIRD: IF YOU HAD 16 CHOCOLATES AND KING PIG ASKED FOR 10, HOW MANY WOULD YOU HAVE LEFT?

THE BLUE BIRDS: 16. WE DON'T LIKE KING PIG.

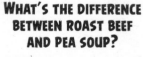

HOW DO YOU STOP AN ELEPHANT FROM STAMPEDING?

You take its stampeder away!

WHAT'S THE DIFFERENCE BETWEEN ROAST BEEF AND PEA SOUP?

Anyone can roast beef.

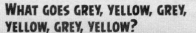

WHAT GOES GREY, YELLOW, GREY, YELLOW, GREY, YELLOW?

An elephant rolling down the hill with a daffodil in its mouth.

WHAT'S A CROCODILE'S FAVOURITE CARD GAME?

Snap!

WHAT DOES A CAT EAT FOR BREAKFAST?

Mice Crispies.

WHERE DO YOU FIND GIANT SNAILS?

At the end of the giant's fingers!

WHAT DO YOU CALL TWO THIEVES?

A pair of nickers!

WHAT FISH ONLY SWIMS AT NIGHT?

A starfish!

AVIAN ANTICS

WHAT SOUND DO KISSING HEDGEHOGS MAKE?
Ouch!

WHAT DO YOU GET IF YOU CROSS AN OWL WITH A SKUNK?
A bird that smells, but doesn't give a hoot!

WHAT BIRD STEALS SOAP FROM YOUR BATH?
Robber duck.

WHAT DO YOU CALL A FUNNY DUCK?
A wise quacker.

WHAT'S A POLYGON?
A dead parrot.

WHY CAN'T AN OWL SING IN THE RAIN?
Because it's too wet to woo!

WHAT KIND OF BIRD LIVES UNDERGROUND?
A mynah bird.

WHAT HAPPENED TO THE OWL WHO TRIPPED OVER?
He felt a bit of twit!

WHAT HAPPENED TO THE OWL WHO TRIPPED OVER AFTER THE FIRST OWL?
He felt a bit of twit, twoo!

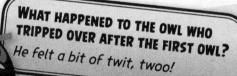

WHAT DO NAUGHTY BIRDS TURN INTO?
Jail birds.

WHY ARE FISH EASY TO WEIGH?
They have their own scales!

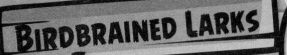

BIRDBRAINED LARKS

WHAT HAPPENED TO THE CHICK THAT WAS NAUGHTY AT SCHOOL?

It got eggspelled!

WHY DID THE SPARROW FLY INTO THE LIBRARY?

It was looking for bookworms.

HOW DID THE CANARY DIE OF FLU?

It flew into a car!

HOW DO HENS DANCE?

Chick to chick!

WHY WAS THE LITTLE BIRD TOLD OFF?

She was always playing practical yolks!

FEATHERBRAINED QUIPS

WHAT BOOKS DO OWLS LIKE?
Hoot-dunnits!

WHAT DID THE POORLY CHICKEN HAVE?
People-pox!

WHICH BIRDS TELL THE BEST JOKES?
Comedi-hens!

WHAT HAS SIX LEGS AND CAN FLY LONG DISTANCES?
Three swallows!

WHAT DO YOU GET IF YOU CROSS A BIRD WITH A FIREWORK?
A Firequacker!

WHY DID THE DUCK MISS HIS TRAIN?

He was doing some last minute quacking!

WHAT IS A PIG'S EXPLANATION FOR THE CREATION OF THE UNIVERSE?

The Pig Bang Theory.

WHY DID THE HEN CROSS THE ROAD, BUT STOP HALF WAY?

She wanted to lay it on the line!

WHO'S THE SMARTEST PIG IN THE WORLD?

Ein-swine

WHY DOES A FLAMINGO LIFT UP ONE LEG?

Because if he lifted up both legs he would fall over!

HOW DO YOU STOP YOUR NOSE FROM RUNNING?

Teach it to hop!

WHAT DO YOU CALL A CRAFTY PIG?

Cunningham!

WHICH FISH IS THE SLEEPIEST?

A kipper.

WHY DID THE SCARECROW WIN AN AWARD?

Because he was out-standing in his field!

WHY IS A TRACTOR MAGIC?

Because it can go down a road and turn into a field!

REALLY FUNNY JOKES ... HONEST

WHAT'S SMARTER THAN A TALKING PIG?
A spelling bee!

WHY COULDN'T THE PIRATE PIG PLAY CARDS?
Because he was sitting on the deck!

WHAT DID THE STAMP SAY TO THE ENVELOPE?
Stick with me and we will go places!

WHY DO BICYCLES FALL OVER?
Because they are two-tired!

WHY DID THE SNAKE CROSS THE ROAD?
To get to the other sssside!

ANGRY BIRDS

A SIDE-SPLITTING,
RIB-TICKLING JOKE BOOK

SNOUTRAGEOUS!

EGMONT
We bring stories to life

First published in Great Britain 2012 by Egmont UK Limited
The Yellow Building, 1 Nicholas Road, London W11 4AN

ISBN 978 1 4052 6657 4
54817/6
Printed in Great Britain